Todd PARR
The I LOVE YOU Book

Megan Tingley Books

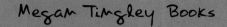

LITTLE, BROWN AND COMPANY
New York • Boston

I love you when you are scared.

I love you when you are brave.

I love you when we are cuddled up close.

I love you when you sleep.

I love you when you don't sleep.

I love you when you are sick.

I love you when you feel better.

I love you when you give me kisses.

I love you when you need hugs.

I love you when you share.

I love you when you are shy.

I love you when you hide my keys.

I love you when you find new friends.

I love you when you are squeaky clean.

I love you when we cook.

I love you when we eat.

Most of all, I love you

just the way you are.

We all need to be loved. ♡

There's enough love for everyone to share. Remember to always love Yourself!

Love,
Todd ♡